Laura's Locket

Laura's Locket

Tima Maria Lacoba

The Dantonville Legacy Series

Published By
Tima Maria Lacoba

Editing by Dionne Lister
Book Cover by JC Clarke thegraphicsshed@gmail.com

Formatting By Paradox Book Covers & Formatting

BOOKS BY TIMA MARIA LACOBA

LAURA'S LOCKET

LAURA

I opened the train window and the cool air rushed in. Although it was January I wanted to breathe in the wintery air. The wind bit my face and made my cheeks tingle. It was refreshing after sitting for an hour in an overheated train compartment. I'd already taken off my coat, scarf and woollen cap, and my angora jumper was scrunched up on the seat.

In the distance, the Mediterranean Sea sparkled in the late afternoon sunshine as our train snaked around the narrow precipice of the southern Italian coastline. Jagged cliffs dropped away inches from the iron tracks that barely clung to the rocky earth.

'Sorrento, next stop,' I said with a smile, then left the window and pulled my bag down from the overhead shelves.

My two best friends, Beth and Angie, also hopped up from their seats to lift their bags down. We'd known each other since seventh grade, and there was rarely a weekend the three of us didn't have a sleepover at one of our homes. At school we'd been nicknamed "The Three Amigos."

And this was our very first trip overseas. I couldn't wait to start our Amalfi holiday.

We linked arms, jumped up and down on the spot and squealed. All through our senior year we'd planned this trip to celebrate the end of high school, worked at part time jobs and saved as much as we could. Our parents made up the shortfall, as did my Aunt Judy, Dad's sister. She chose our hotels and had even paid for mine.

I glanced out the window just as we passed a secluded cove and the gentle undulations of an inflated palm tree close to the shoreline caught my eye.

'Look at this. An artificial tropical island!' I said and pointed. 'Must be anchored to a rock below the waves or something.'

Beth and Angie squeezed in next to me and stuck their heads out the window.

'A fake palm tree. That's classic!' Beth said while clawing away tendrils of her long, black hair the wind had whipped around her face.

Beth's family had migrated from Mumbai when she was three, and their house was only a street away from mine in Earlwood. Her dark exotic looks were in stark contrast to my coppery locks and lavender-coloured eyes. I envied her being able to stay out in the strong Australian sun, whereas my pale skin turned pink within five minutes.

'Does it belong to a resort or something?' she added. 'Wonder if there're more?' Her ebony eyes scanned the coastline ahead.

It seemed so out of place. The beach was empty: no deck chairs, umbrellas or the usual summer paraphernalia. But then, it was January, and all the resorts were closed. Perhaps this was one thing they'd forgotten to pack away for the winter.

'You know, Laura, I'm still surprised your parents let you go. They've got to be the most over-protective people I've ever met,' Angie said, a thick, faux fur hat tucked so low over her curly brown hair I could barely see her eyes.

Even before we had purchased our airline tickets, Angie had splashed out on the latest winter fashions. That the hat was too big for her didn't matter—it was "in!" Masking her eyes as it did, I worried she could trip and hurt herself.

'Well, it's only-child syndrome, so I can kind of understand,' I added quietly. It had taken a lot of persuading on my part. I'd asked my aunt Judy to talk to them too. She and Dad were close, although I knew she wasn't keen on my trip either. 'But Angie and Beth'll be with me. I'm not going alone,' I'd told her. 'You know them. Pleeease?' It worked.

'That's cos you look so young. No one'd guess you're an adult. I reckon you'll have to pull out your passport every time you order a drink,' Angie said as she pushed the hat back off her brow for the umpteenth time.

I stuck my tongue out at her and she laughed. So did I.

'They're probably worried you'll meet some foreign guy, and won't want to come home,' Beth said.

I shook my head. 'No way!' I had no intention of doing anything of the sort, but the prospect of meeting a hot Italian guy was exciting. I was on holidays, so why not have a little romance? The problem is my handicap. It's not a physical one, more like a weird genetic anomaly—I age slowly, very slowly. At eighteen, in the prime of life, I hadn't got my period yet. And, I was still a virgin. *How embarrassing!*

'We're here!' Angie squealed. The train rounded another bend and began to slow. She leant her head further out, gripping her oversized, fur hat. 'It's so pretty.'

Clusters of red-roofed houses and three-to-four-storey buildings honeycombed the cliff side all the way to the sea. In the marina, only a few boats bobbed on the waves, large luxury yachts among them.

Beth and I tried to see past Angie, but the wind stung my eyes. I flopped back into my seat and threw on my jumper. 'C'mon you guys, we'll be there any minute. Better get your stuff together.'

'Should we get a taxi or walk to the hotel?' Angie's voice sounded muffled as she struggled into her shocking-pink anorak.

'No way we're going to lose you in a crowd wearing that thing,' I teased.

Angie laughed and dipped her knee in a mock curtsy. 'No way, matey. Besides, it's *so* this season.'

I rolled my eyes, but I admired Angie's love of bright colours and her ability to wear them with such unabashed confidence.

'Laura, you've got the map.' Beth took charge. 'How far's the hotel from the station?' She checked her reflection in the aisle window and adjusted her beret.

I retrieved the Lonely Planet Guidebook from my coat pocket. 'Um… on here it looks really close; down the hill from the station. Fifteen to twenty minutes to the Piazza Tasso maybe?'

'Okay, walk then?' She turned to face us, eyebrows raised. We'd elected Beth as our unofficial leader, being the oldest. At nineteen she was already engaged to her long-time boyfriend, Ashley. She was even on the Pill.

Angie looked at me and shrugged. 'Sure. We've been sitting for ages.'

She had a point. After the first twelve hours of the twenty-two hour flight from Sydney, the novelty had worn off and I couldn't wait to land. At the Bangkok stopover, I practically ran from one end of the terminal to the other; not so much to catch our connecting flight, but for some exercise.

The train stopped, and we followed the other passengers along the platform. Heads down, faces concealed in scarves and bundled up against the cold, they dispersed leaving us staring at a sparsely populated square—the Piazza Angelina Lauro.

In less than fifteen minutes we stood before a set of tall, scrolled wrought iron gates, behind which we glimpsed an imposing, terracotta-coloured building. The sign read: Grand Excelsior Vittoria Hotel.

It would be our home for the next three days.

* * *

Several hours later, we'd unpacked, napped and now sought food. It was dark, but the piazza teemed with people, their faces illuminated by the decorative street lanterns that swayed in the evening breeze. It was magical. The only drawback was the local boys who whistled and followed us down the street as if they had nothing better to do.

Angie and I giggled, but Beth shooed them away. I did my best to ignore them by looking in the shop windows, as we explored the old part of town, and putting my hands in my coat pockets when they tried to grab hold of them. My stomach grumbled in anticipation as the enticing aromas of cooked garlic and olive oil, interspersed with the sweet scent of lemoncello, wafted from each café and restaurant we passed.

One of the boys, with enticing brown eyes and his dark hair curling over his collar, approached me, whispered something in Italian, and kissed me full on the mouth. I pushed him back.

That's when *he* appeared.

Tall, commanding and with his straight blonde hair flowing over his shoulders, he seemed to materialise from nowhere.

The boys backed off. The one who kissed me, turned and ran. The others followed.

'They won't bother you, now,' said the man. His deep blue eyes transfixed me—I couldn't look away. He gazed at me, as if waiting for a response, but I was speechless. It's not everyday a girl comes face to face with such a beautiful man.

Angie nudged me with her elbow.

'Ah, thank you,' I finally managed.

'My pleasure!' He smiled, and my insides turned to jelly. When he lifted my hand to his lips I resisted the urge to sigh. It was such an old-fashioned, yet romantic gesture. No one had ever kissed my hand before. His gaze remained on my face, and even though people walked by, I barely noticed—there was only him.

Beth coughed. 'Okay, let's get going. Time for dinner.'

'I'd recommend that place over there.' The man pointed to his left—La Dolce Vita. 'I hear it's good.' His velvety voice had a slight accent, not Italian. French perhaps? 'By the way, my name's Philippe.'

He is French!

'I'm Laura and this is Beth and Angie,' I indicated my friends.

'Charmed.' He inclined his head.

'Would you like to join us?' Angie asked. She looked at him eagerly from beneath the brim of her hat, hazel eyes sparkling.

Please say, yes!

He seemed about to answer, when his gaze slanted past, to somewhere behind us, and his brow creased in a frown. He hesitated before saying, 'Regrettably, no. I'm... expected elsewhere. Please excuse me.' With a final glance at me, Philippe disappeared into the crowd.

The three of us stared after him. Angie let out a sigh. 'First day in Europe and we meet the hottest of hotties!' She then turned to me and slapped my arm. Her hat had slipped further down and now sat just above her nose, which was pink from the cold. 'Why didn't you ask him to stay? It was obvious he liked you.'

'He was just being polite, and besides, I didn't know what to say.'

'Being polite? I don't think so!' She grinned. 'He couldn't get his eyes off you, Laura.'

She and Beth exchanged glances. 'Ooooh!' They sing-songed.

I rolled my eyes and started to walk in the direction of the restaurant Philippe suggested. But secretly I was thrilled and hoped we'd bump into one another before the girls and I left Sorrento. Beth and Angie caught up with me and linked their arms through mine.

'You know, that was a bit weird,' Beth stated.

'What was?' I asked.

'The way he shows up like some kind of white knight, rescues you from a bunch of silly boys, stares at you like he wants to eat you, and then disappears.'

I laughed. 'Eat me?'

'Yeah, like this!' Angie leapt in front of me, pushed her hat back off her face and gave me the smouldering-eyes look. 'I will eat you, my little chicken!' she said in a mock French accent.

Beth burst out laughing. 'Classic!'

I pulled Angie's hat back down onto her nose and laughed, too.

'Did you see those guys' faces?' Beth said. 'The way they backed away from him.' She was always the thinker. 'What if he's mafia or something?'

I hadn't thought of that. Beth could be right. He had the air of authority, and his clothes were well-cut; definitely designer wear. But then, many Europeans were well dressed.

We stopped in front of the restaurant and looked through the windows. The place was full. 'He doesn't have to be Mafia. What if he's a cop?' I suggested.

Angie pushed open the glass doors. The delicious scent of garlic bread hit my nostrils and I forgot Philippe. This place was popular, and just as I thought we would have to go elsewhere, one table was vacated. We made a beeline for it. I chewed on a breadstick as we decided our order and absently glanced out the window—and almost choked.

His face stared back at me!

My heart leapt. I blinked and he was gone. I blinked again. Had I imagined it? Not likely. Maybe he changed his mind?

The restaurant door opened and an elderly couple walked in. My heart dropped.

Get a grip! It had only been a chance meeting. The probability of bumping into him again was so remote it didn't bear thinking about. Yet, deep down, I hoped we would.

* * *

The next day we were on the train to Pompeii. It was the first item on our to-do list. Soon we were standing in the once-thriving hub of that dead city—the Forum—an ancient plaza that had hummed with people, now eerily silent as the shadow of Vesuvius fell over the ancient temple of Saturn.

I stared up at it in horrified fascination.

Being winter, few tourists were about. I tried to visualise the terrified chaos of the people who had once lived here. The preserved casts of children and even infants who had died that day two thousand years ago brought tears to my eyes.

I thought of Naples where our plane had landed. It was situated at the base of the deadly mountain. 'You know if Vesuvius ever erupts again, Naples will become the next Pompeii.' I said.

'Great!' Beth glared up at the volcano. 'Better not happen while we're here.'

'When was the last time it did?' Angie asked.

I flipped through the pages of our tour booklet. '1940s.'

'Seriously? That's not that long ago.' She stuck her face right up against the glass barrier where a whole family group was preserved. When she drew away, an impression of her forehead and nose remained for a brief moment.

'That's so sad,' I said. 'Those poor people didn't make it out.'

'Gives me the creeps,' Beth said, pulling her red coat tighter and buttoning it up. 'Wanna leave for Positano tomorrow?'

'No!' I said too quickly. Philippe's face appeared in my mind and I wondered where he was and what he was doing? If we left now, I might miss a chance meeting. My friends looked at me, then at each other and shrugged.

That night, we dined again in the same restaurant. My eyes lingered on the window, but I didn't see his face. Nor did I glimpse him in the streets. It began to rain, and as we ran through the hotel entrance, it was pelting down.

* * *

Tap! Tap! The sound woke me. *Tap!* I sat up, rubbed the sleep from my eyes and checked my watch. One a.m. The sound came from the direction of the glass balcony doors. The moon was full, and by its light I caught the glint of something hanging in the window. It appeared to be attached to a dark object stuck to the glass. The wind outside buffeted it against the pane. That's what was making the tapping sound.

My heart jumped into my throat. Was it a cat burglar?

I pushed aside the feather quilt, threw on my dressing gown and padded to the balcony. I stood and debated whether to open the doors and retrieve the object.

Tap! Tap!

Curiosity won. I turned the handle, opened the door enough to retrieve the object, and quickly shut it again. I held a white card from which dangled a spiral seashell, on a silk ribbon. Its pearly surface caught the pearly glint of moonlight.

I switched on my bedside lamp.

Laura,
We met yesterday on the street and I would
like to see you again.
I'm downstairs in the lobby.
Please come.
Philippe

My stomach clenched. How did he know where I was staying? Had he followed us? Maybe Beth was right, and he was in the mafia, or... or some kind of psycho.

I groaned inwardly and sent up a silent prayer. *Please, don't let him be a stalker!*

Well, there was only one way to find out.

I promised Mum and Dad, and my aunt, I wouldn't go anywhere alone. Did the hotel foyer count? I'd still be in the same building, so technically I wouldn't be on my own, and there were bound to be night staff around.

I dressed in minutes, opened my bedroom door and crept out into the lounge. Beth's door was slightly ajar as I tiptoed from the suite.

Philippe stood facing me when the elevator doors opened. My breath caught in my throat at the sight of him. His shoulder-length blonde hair was tied back with a black ribbon, and the black leather jacket emphasised the width of his shoulders.

He took my hand, kissed it and said, 'Thank you for coming. I know it's very late for you,' as he led me into the grand lobby where soothing, romantic music was piped through the speakers. No one else was about except the night clerk at the reception desk, who glanced up briefly as we strolled past.

C'mon, Laura, find your tongue! 'Ah, don't you sleep?'

'I had… work to complete. Can I get you a drink?' he asked, indicating a plush, brocaded seat for me.

'No, thank you.' My heart hammered in my chest, but I tried to appear calm. I smiled and kept my hands behind my back so he couldn't see how nervous I was. 'How did you know my hotel?'

He sat opposite me. 'A close friend owns several here. I simply asked him to find out where a beautiful girl called Laura and her two friends were staying.'

'All that trouble to find me? Why not slide your card under my door?'

'You may not have seen it till the morning, and I couldn't wait.' His smile was devastating, and it took a while before my pulse returned to normal. He was so self-assured, and thought nothing of waking me at one in the morning. Were all European men like that?

'How did you get up there?' I asked. 'It's four storeys up.'

'My secret.' He sat back in his chair and smoothed back his hair like a preening cat, his sensuous lips curled in a smile.

My heart lurched into my mouth as the thought of him being a cat burglar entered my mind. What if he regularly scaled walls and climbed along rooftops to enter the rooms of rich tourists?

'Are you a cat burglar?' The words were out of my mouth before I could stop them, and I clamped my hand over my mouth.

He laughed, a genuine deep-throated chuckle. 'No, I promise you I am not a cat burglar or any such thing.' He stopped and regarded me a while. 'Your candour is refreshing.'

A polite way of putting it! I have a habit of saying what other people only think. 'Who are you, Philippe? What is your last name?'

'Reynard. My home is in Paris. A friend asked me to join him here for a few days and I wasn't going to come, but now… I'm glad I did.' He gazed at me so intently my stomach bunched into knots.

'We're, ah… leaving in a few days.' I wasn't sure whether to tell him our next destination.

'Amalfi Coast?'

I'm sure my jaw dropped. 'How did you know?'

'Sorrento's usually the starting point for most tourists on their way there. Positano, is it?' He leaned forward and eased the solid, wooden coffee table that separated us out of the way with his foot. *It must be lighter than it looks,* I thought. 'Where will you be staying?' he asked.

'I really shouldn't tell you. I... know nothing about you. I shouldn't even be sitting here with you.'

He chuckled again. 'Quite right to be cautious.' Then he sobered and grasped my hands in his. 'But you have nothing to fear from me. I would never hurt you.' There was such earnestness in his voice and eyes, I wanted to believe him... did believe him.

'We're staying at the—'

'Tell me the night before you leave. That way we must keep seeing each other until then.' Philippe had released one of my hands and lightly pressed a finger over my lips. He then slowly traced the outline of my mouth, his eyes holding mine captive as every nerve in my body tingled.

I was lost for words. No, mesmerized. How could a girl not be flattered, when the best looking guy she's ever seen was asking her out? And he was a man: elegant, charming and sophisticated, and so unlike the boys I'd known in high school. I guessed he was at least in his mid twenties. I glanced at his mouth and wondered what kissing him would be like; how his lips would taste.

He inhaled long and deep, then gave me a broad smile. Had he read my mind? I averted my eyes and pulled my hand from his grasp as heat flooded my cheeks.

The piped music in the foyer now swelled, as though on cue, and a mellow male voice began to sing. Philippe stood and offered me his hand. I accepted, and we danced, arm in arm, swaying to the music. He held me tighter with each new tune. I inhaled the spice and leather of his scent and brushed my cheek against his.

My heart fluttered as the dreamed-of holiday romance had begun. I wanted to enjoy it; for my sensible side warned me this couldn't last. He lived in France and I lived in Australia. This was probably as much a holiday romance for him as it was for me. Another thought occurred to me—maybe he did this often, with other tourist girls. Maybe he was married with half-a-dozen kids.

'Anything wrong?' He pulled back and gazed down at me.

'I... I don't know you, Philippe. Are, um... are you... married?' *Please, God, don't let him be married!*

'So that's what's worrying you.' He chuckled. 'No, I'm not. No woman has a claim on me.'

It was a strange way to assure me, yet I instantly relaxed and rested my head on his shoulder.

'That's better,' he murmured in my ear, then brushed my hair aside. His cool lips skimmed the length of my throat.

A warm sensation rippled through me and as we continued to sway to the rhythmic sounds of the piped music, our bodies seemed to meld into each other. A perfect fit. We were the only two people in the world, and when the music stopped, we continued to dance to the music within us. And we talked. He was interested in everything about me—my education and friends. Did I have a boyfriend back home?

'Not a steady one,' I replied. Apart from one I'd dated in my senior year, I'd never been that keen on the boys in my school. They were so immature.

'I'm a portrait artist.' He stopped and gazed intently at me. 'Let me paint you, Laura. Beauty such as yours should be immortalized.'

My breath left me and I longed to say yes. Yet, an inner voice whispered caution. 'I don't know.'

'Promise me you'll think about it.'

'Okay.'

'Now I'll take you back to your room. I've kept you up long enough.'

'I'm not tired.' I could have stayed in his arms all night.

'You will be in the morning.' He trailed his hand slowly down the side of my face and neck as his eyes held mine. His head suddenly swiveled to the side and he frowned.

'What is it?' I asked.

'Nothing. I… thought I heard something.' Whatever it was, it had altered his mood. 'Come. Back to your room.' Philippe took my hand and escorted me to the door of my suite. 'Meet me tomorrow night?'

'Same time?'

He shook his head. 'I have a confession. I only asked you at such a late hour to see if you'd come, and you did.' He gave me a slow, seductive smile.

'Only out of curiosity,' I replied in response to slight smugness of his tone.

'Curiosity satisfied?' He leaned toward me, his gaze riveted on my mouth.

My throat dried. 'Um… I'll let you know tomorrow night.'

Philippe chuckled. 'Does eleven suit?'

'Why so late? Can't we meet for lunch?' Could I keep sneaking out late at night and not tell Beth and Angie? What if something happened and I wasn't there? They'd panic. I couldn't do it to them.

'I'm sorry, but… I have work to do. Only my nights are free.'

'Oh.' I leant back against the door of my suite wondering what to do.

Philippe braced his hands on either side of my head and waited. His face so close to mine, our breaths mingled, and my heart hammered. My gaze wandered to his mouth again. I could almost taste his lips and wanted him to kiss me. But he didn't.

'You can't or you won't?' he said.

His comment stung and my gaze shot back to his eyes. What I saw in those blue orbs both frightened and exhilarated me—an unfamiliar intensity, and hurt, desire and a whole host of other things I didn't understand. It was irresistible, yet if I gave in, it would also be irresponsible.

'Yes or no, Laura?' His voice took on a pleading tone.

'Yes, all right. Tomorrow night at eleven.'

He smiled, grasped my hands and brought them to his lips.

The sensible part of me thought of a thousand reasons why I should say no, but I'd stopped listening.

* * *

The next day the rain had stopped and the seas were calm enough for us to take the ferry to Capri. As we wandered through the remains of Emperor Tiberius's palace, admiring the beautiful wall paintings and statues, I yawned. Several times. I couldn't take them in. Not only was I tired but my mind was on Philippe, and our rendezvous tonight. I experienced a thrill every time I thought of it—which was often.

'What's with you, Laura?' Angie said. We were back in our hotel room and I crashed onto my bed. 'You've been vague all day.'

'Sorry, I'm just… tired, that's all.'

'Why?'

I grabbed the pillow and shoved it over my head, mumbling, 'Late nights.' Since it was the truth, I didn't hiccup, which I tended to do whenever I tried to lie.

That night we ate in the hotel restaurant, and while Beth and Angie took to the dance floor at the disco afterwards, I excused myself and sauntered back to our suite to try to get a few hours sleep.

My wristwatch alarm went off. It was nearly eleven. I'd changed into another outfit before going to bed, so all I needed to do was comb my hair and brush my teeth. Would he kiss me tonight? The butterflies in my stomach danced at the thought.

The lounge area of our suite was dark when I stepped out of my room. The doors to the girls' rooms were closed, so it was hard to know whether they were asleep or still out dancing.

I guess I can always take a peek!' I thought as I tiptoed to Beth's room and placed my ear against the door. Not a sound. 'Beth?' I whispered. No answer. *They must be burning up the dance floor.* Taking a deep breath, I left our suite and ran down the corridor toward the elevator.

Philippe was waiting. He was in black leather, and his beaming smile erased any concerns I had about keeping my meetings with him a secret from my two best friends. He had a bike helmet under one arm, and held another one. 'Put this on, Laura. We're going for a ride.'

'Out of the hotel?' I assumed we'd stay in the guest lounge. The cashmere sweater, tiered woollen skirt and boots I wore weren't suitable for a wintery night jaunt on a motorbike.

'I don't think they'd let me ride it in here, do you?' He gave me a heart-stopping, lopsided smile.

Before I had the chance to reply, Philippe grabbed my hand and made for the exit. A silver motorcycle stood beneath the gleam of a full moon. Its sleek lines resembled a powerful animal ready to spring.

'Yours?' I asked.

'Mine.' He removed his black leather jacket and placed it around my shoulders. 'Put this on.'

I slipped my arms into the sleeves, still warm from his body, and hugged it to me. 'Philippe, I don't think this is a good idea.' A tinge of fear crept through me. It was one thing to meet in the confines of the hotel, but another entirely to go with him somewhere unknown. After all, I'd only known him a couple of days, or nights, to be precise. I also remembered the promise I made my parents.

Philippe took my face between his hands. 'You're afraid. Don't be. As I said last night, I would never harm you or expose you to danger. Please, trust me.'

I desperately wanted to, but the sensible part of my brain was screaming at me to turn around and go back to my room.

'If I promise to bring you back here within a few hours, walking through these doors,' he pointed to the hotel's sliding glass doors, 'and safely in bed by three, will you come?'

There was a deep yearning in his eyes I couldn't resist, and somewhere within me, I knew he spoke the truth; that I was safe with him. I stopped listening to the sensible part of me. 'All right, I'll come.'

His lips lightly brushed mine and my pulse went into hyperdrive. 'Put the helmet on,' he said. 'There's a place I want to show you.'

'Aren't you cold in just that T-shirt?' I asked while I buckled the chinstraps.

'Don't feel it. Ready?' The engine roared to life.

'Ready.' Wrapped warmly within Philippe's jacket, I straddled the seat behind him, slid my arms around his chest and felt the stone-hard muscles beneath the cotton fabric. I inhaled the scent of leather and spice—Philippe's scent.

We sped into the night, through narrow cobblestone streets and along the serpentine, cliff-side road. He handled the bike with such confidence, managing the twists and turns with ease in the dark, I found myself enjoying the freedom of the open road, even the biting cold wind on my face.

A few minutes later, Philippe slowed down, turned off the road onto a lookout, switched off the engine and cut the headlight.

For a moment we were swallowed up by the dark until my eyes adjusted to the silvery glow thrown by the full moon. There it hung, like a celestial pearl, its ribbon of light casting a liquid trail over the sea. It appeared close enough to touch. Just a step away. Only the crashing of the waves on the shore, far below, revealed how close we stood to the edge.

I inhaled deeply, letting the salty flavor fill my lungs. 'It's beautiful,' I said, as I removed my bike helmet.

'Smugglers used these coves for centuries. There are caves all along this coast. But that's not what I brought you here to see.' He swung off the seat, lifted me off the bike and pulled me into his arms. My heart thundered in my chest as his eyes bored into mine. He brushed the back of his knuckles down the side of my face. 'Soon, I'll kiss you the way you should be kissed.'

My knees almost turned to marshmallow at his words, and my breath stopped somewhere between my lungs and my throat.

'Not much further now, but there are many steps. I don't want you to trip.' He hoisted me into his arms and began to descend a steep set of stairs leading down to the beach.

'What about you?' I asked. If he tripped we'd both go for a ride.

He laughed, kissed me on the nose and took the stairs two at a time. I couldn't look and instead I gazed up at the stream of unfamiliar northern stars that blinked in and out of the clouds.

When he reached the bottom, Philippe lowered me to my feet. Less than a hundred feet away was a small hut, its windows alight with a cozy glow. With my hand in his, Philippe led the way, to what I assumed was, a fisherman's hut.

There was no one else around; no winking lights from yachts out to sea; no glare from headlights of passing cars; no human voices. Apart from the crunch of our boots on the pebbled shore, the lapping of the waves on the beach—and the erratic thumping of my heart—all was silent. We were alone. Yet, for some inexplicable reason, I wasn't afraid.

He opened the door to reveal a fire in the grate. On the wooden table and along the windowsills, thick white candles spluttered in the draught from the open door. Fishing nets were strung across the ceiling and walls. The aroma of burning wood mingled with a strong scent of the sea.

'You did all this?' I asked.

'I wanted it to be perfect,' he said, and his lips grazed my neck.

My body shivered in anticipation. Was this the night? But why here? 'Why so far away?'

'No interruptions.' He closed the door behind me and turned the key.

My heart gave another thump.

A coloured rug covered the floor. Philippe knelt down and drew me after him. 'I have something for you.' From his pocket he extracted a small, blue silk bag. I could see an outline, but couldn't make it out. He untied the string and lifted out a silver, filigree heart-shaped locket.

I sucked in a breath.

Philippe leant toward me and placed it around my neck. 'So you'll never forget me,' he said, then pulled me close and kissed me. His lips were soft and warm; gentle yet demanding. He lowered me onto the rug and pressed my mouth closer to his, all the while caressing my cheek with one hand. 'Have you ever been French kissed?' he asked after a while.

'Yeah… kind of.' My voice shook. The boys I'd let kiss me in high school had tried that, and it disgusted me. Their wet, slobbery attempts at thrusting their tongues into my mouth had filled me with revulsion. I wasn't keen to repeat the experience.

'Obviously unsuccessfully.' His gaze burned into mine. 'Let me show you how it's done.'

Philippe angled my head, placed his mouth over mine again and deftly parted my lips. His tongue glided over my bottom lip, then the top, before venturing into my mouth, seeking admittance and a response. My tongue tentatively rose to meet his, and Philippe caught it.

I never thought I'd enjoy the feel of a man's tongue, gliding and sliding over mine, tasting, tantalizing me, and leave me begging for more. How much time we spent locked in each other's arms, I don't know, but my lips were beginning to grow numb from all the attention they received. Philippe's hand caressed my breast beneath my sweater. He lifted his head and gazed down at me. 'I love you, Laura. Do you think you can love me back?'

His declaration took me by surprise. 'So soon? I mean... I don't know. I've never been in love before.' Did constantly thinking about him, and not being able to concentrate on anything but him; wanting to be in his company only, all the time, constituted being in love? Then maybe I was.

Philippe chuckled, 'You're so innocent.' His expression changed—sobered. He rose, went over to the table and blew out the candles. 'I promised to take you home by three.'

The candles on the windowsills had burned low. Although the fire in the grate was still strong, the scent of the burning wood mingled with the smell of the fishing nets. It was pungent, but I didn't mind. I could stay all night, but then how would I explain my absence to Beth and Angie? They'd be shocked—as would my family if they knew. I had to get back, yet Philippe had me spellbound and my conflicting emotions were waging a battle.

I sat up. 'I know. My friends mustn't see me sneaking back to our suite. I haven't told them about you.'

'What are your plans for the day?'

'Just hanging around Sorrento. It's our last night before we head off to Positano.'

'I'm sorry, you'll be tired tomorrow.'

'I'm wide awake now!' I gazed up at him longingly while trying to blink away the heaviness of my eyelids.

He chuckled, came back to my side and kissed me again, long and deeply. Although my breath left me, I didn't want it to end. But it did. Philippe rose in one fluid movement, pulled me after him and held me tight for a moment before releasing me. I wondered why he hadn't tried to sleep with me, and I didn't want to ask why. In some way I was relieved. I wasn't ready.

On the ride back to the hotel, I leant my head against his back. In spite of my earlier words, I was growing tired. My eyes were closed as Philippe steered the motorbike along the quiet streets.

As on the previous two nights, he escorted me to my suite on the fourth floor of the hotel. 'Tomorrow night?' he asked.

I didn't know if I could keep this up, existing on a couple of hours sleep per night. Yet, I couldn't help myself. The days were too long till I could see him again.

'Tomorrow night.'

He took my face in his hands and kissed me goodnight. I watched him walk away before closing the door.

* * *

'Where have you been?' Beth stood in the lounge, hands on her hips. Her eyes brimmed with tears.

'We've been worried sick, Laura!' Angie said. 'Beth rang your aunt—'

'I didn't have the courage to let your parents know, so I rang your Aunt Judy instead. She gave me her number before we left.'

My stomach sank.

'I was ready to call the police!' Beth sank onto the sofa and burst into tears.

I ran over and crouched on the floor in front of her. 'I'm so sorry, so sorry. I didn't mean to worry you—'

'Why'd you do it then?' Angie cried before joining Beth on the sofa. 'When we came in from the disco, we saw your bedroom door closed and dark so we thought you were asleep. If not for the fire alarm—'

'You had a fire?'

'It was a false alarm, but we had to be evacuated anyway. The staff knocked on everyone's doors to get them out. I raced into your room and you weren't there!' She glared at me. 'The hotel staff have been running around looking for you!'

I buried my face in my hands at the sickening realization of what I had done to my friends. No amount of apology could atone for this, and a hot blush scalded my cheeks. I couldn't blame them if they wouldn't want to continue our trip after this.

'Where were you, Laura?' I looked up to see Beth wiping her eyes. The hurt I saw in them broke my heart and I began to cry.

'I'm so sorry… I… it was stupid of me not to leave a note or something, I know… but he—'

'He?' Angie said.

I nodded. 'Philippe.'

Angie's eyes widened, and she shook her head. 'You've been with him, all this time?'

I nodded again. She threw her hands in the air and groaned. I told them everything and showed them Philippe's note with the attached shell. After I finished, Beth rose and rang my aunt. She held the phone out to me. 'You talk to her.'

They sat and watched.

I took a deep breath. Aunt Judy answered. 'It's me, Laura. Everything's okay. I'm so sorry to have worried you.' Her words were terse but I could tell it stemmed from concern. I could sense the tension on the other end; hear it in her voice and her disappointment. I recounted to her what I'd told the girls. She asked for his name. I told her. There was a few seconds silence on her side before she spoke again. She made me promise not to meet with him again; not without Beth and Angie being present.

I promised.

'She okay?' Angie asked. 'You've gone white, Laura.' I nodded. That's all I was capable of doing. That, and swiping away my tears. 'What did she say?'

'Made me promise not to meet him again unless you two are with me.' The tears kept coming.

'You've always been the most sensible one,' Beth exclaimed. 'This isn't like you, Laura.'

'Are you in love with him?' Angie asked. 'Because if you are it… kinda makes sense. Love makes you do stupid things. Remember me and Greg?' She grimaced.

Angie and Greg had started dating in Year Eleven. He'd gotten his driver's license and was into drag racing. Angie hated the smell of petrol, but she was besotted by him. He took her for a race. The car flipped and she ended up in hospital. She wasn't allowed to see him unless one of her parents was with them. A few months later they broke up.

'I don't know how I feel about him! But I so want to see him again, and I told him I would—tomorrow night, and now I promised Aunt Judy….' I bit my lip and fingered the locket around my neck.

'I don't remember you having a locket like that.' Angie pointed to it. 'Nice.

'Philippe gave it to me.'

Angie and Beth exchanged glances.

'Can I have a look?' Beth held out her hand. I undid the clasp and handed it to her. She opened the locket and examined it from every angle.

'What are you looking for?' I asked.

'Drugs, you idiot,' Beth replied. 'Only a few grams can land you in jail in a foreign country.'

A horrible churning started in my stomach. I didn't want to believe Philippe would do something like that. But what did I know? I'd only met him two nights ago. I knew nothing about him or where he was staying. He didn't even give me a contact number. Was I really such a naïve idiot?

'It's clean.' Beth handed the locket back. 'Maybe he is okay.' She crouched on the floor next to me and gave me a tight hug. 'Don't ever do something like that again!'

I hugged her back. 'What'll I do, Beth?'

Angie joined us and threw her arms around both of us. 'Beth and I'll go – as your body guards.'

'Just as you agreed with your aunt,' Beth said.

How on earth will I face him? I thought. But a promise was a promise.

* * *

We spent the day shopping in Sorrento, and although I tried to keep my mind off Philippe, it wasn't possible. The closer the time came to our meeting, the tenser I became.

At eleven Beth and Angie accompanied me to the ground floor. They intended to sit inconspicuously in the public lounge and keep an eye on me—or rather, on Philippe. No romantic trips out of the hotel.

My heart beat double time as the elevator slowly descended.

The doors slid open to an empty lobby. On the last two occasions he'd been waiting for me.

'Laura, we'll be over there.' Beth pointed to a set of sofas. Angie waved as they moved off.

My nervousness returned. How was I going to explain the situation to Philippe? Would he understand? I checked my watch. He'd never been late before. I paced the lobby. Half an hour later Philippe still hadn't appeared.

Where was he? I turned to where the girls sat, and shrugged, then I began to worry. 'Something's wrong. He's never been late before.'

'Wait a bit longer. Maybe he's been held up,' Beth suggested, stifling a yawn.

We waited till midnight. Angie had fallen asleep on the sofa. I was panicking. 'He's had an accident,' I said. 'We should tell the man at reception to ring the hospital and find out.'

'Laura, are you sure he hasn't just stood you up?'

'No!' I tugged on the locket around my neck. 'Would he give me this if he wasn't going to show?'

Beth chewed on her lower lip—a sure sign that she was thinking. 'Okay, you go to the front desk and I'll wake Angie.'

I raced to the reception counter and hoped the night clerk understood English. He did. There was only one hospital in Sorrento, the Santa Maria Misericordia—if there had been an accident, Philippe would be taken there. He kindly rang them.

'Philippe Reynard,' I told him. 'He's French, from Paris.'

The man smiled at me as he waited for the hospital to check their records. 'Ah, grazie. Buonna Notte.' He ended the call. 'I'm sorry, signorina, but no one with that name has been admitted.'

'And there've been no accidents… people taken to another hospital elsewhere?'

'No, signorina. It's been a quiet season. I'm sorry. Maybe he will ring you tomorrow.' He gave me one of those sympathetic looks, reserved for tourist-girls-stood-up-by-local-guys.

'Thank you.' I didn't know what else to say.

Beth placed her arm around my shoulders. 'No luck?'

I shook my head. It didn't make sense. Was he suddenly called away, and didn't have time to leave a note? We were scheduled to leave tomorrow. He knew that. Perhaps he'd contact me in Positano. But I never told him the name of the hotel.

Angie yawned, pushed her curly hair off her face and said, 'C'mon Laura, let's go to bed. It's been a killer night… or morning… whatever.'

'I don't understand!' I cried. 'He said he'd be here. Why isn't he? What if he's lying hurt, somewhere on the street – in a coma?' I clutched the filigree locket tightly in my palm hoping it would somehow magically summon him to me.

'Oh sweetie, don't torture yourself.' Beth hugged me. 'Some men… well, they see a gorgeous girl like you, and it's like a game to them—a challenge.'

I pulled out of her embrace and vehemently shook my head. 'No, not him!' *It can't be.*

'Laura, how do you know he isn't married or something?' Angie stated.

'Because he told me he wasn't! Said no woman had a claim on him.' *Could he have lied?* Acid burned in my throat.

Angie said gently, 'Men lie. They do it all the time. Remember the guys at school?'

I shook my head again. *No, no, no.* Could it all have been just a joke to him? A deep hollow pit opened up in my stomach. The acid burned deeper.

There wasn't much left of the night when we returned to our suite. Sleep eluded me, and I tossed and turned from one side of the bed to the other. My mind replayed every moment since we'd met, lingering longest on the romantic interlude in the fisherman's hut last night. It couldn't have been a game to him. Could it?

I closed my eyes and once again felt the firmness of his lips on mine, the strength of his arms, saw the deep blue of his eyes as they gazed into mine.

I tucked the note he'd left on my window a couple of nights ago under my pillow, hoping it would bring him to me in my dreams, at least. The silver locket was still around my neck. I vowed never to take it off, and as my fingers traced the outline of its surface, my heart splintered and the tears I'd held back cascaded down my face onto the pillow.

The next day I left a note for Philippe with the hotel clerk—just in case.

I wasn't in the mood to talk when we boarded the train for Positano, and even as we pulled out of the station, I hung out of the window hoping his tall figure was among the crowds.

'Close it, Laura. It's cold,' Angie said. Her tone was clipped, and there were dark circles under her eyes.

The sun shone brightly, not a cloud in the sky. It could have been summer, but for the icy wind blowing in from the sea.

Beth linked her arm through mine. 'Amalfi Coast, Laura. You've been looking forward to it.'

I nodded and blindly stared at the passing scenery.

* * *

Four weeks later…

The crowd on the university campus jostled me and Angie as I tried to find the clubs to join. We had barely returned from our trip to Italy when our enrolment papers arrived. Each of us had managed to get into the courses we'd chosen, but Beth's was at another university, on the other side of the city.

Angie and I clutched our university ID cards and excitedly checked out the myriad of campus societies who'd set up marquees on the lawn in the main quadrangle. Each had groups of people milling around or standing in a queue to sign up.

The range of choices was mind-boggling.

'Okay if we split and I go over there?' Angie pointed to a white marquee with the sign, "Eggheads and Boffins Science Club." Science was her love and I knew she looked forward to a career in Food Technology.

'Go, have fun, Angie. I'm fine. I promise.' I smiled and crossed my heart. *No more moping over Philippe,* I angrily told myself.

She grinned at me. 'Meet you here, in this spot, in an hour.' I gave her a quick hug and she joined the queue. She'd worn a bright orange mini-skirt that stood out like a beacon—so I'd find her anywhere should we get separated.

I took a deep breath and scanned the campus. There was a particular group I wanted to join after seeing their advert in the Campus News—one of a whole bundle of papers in our enrolment package.

As I fingered the locket around my neck, Philippe's face sprang into my mind—the hurt of never hearing from him again still fresh. Each night I had waited for a phone call, a note, anything. Maybe the girls were right, and I'd been just a game to him, a fun way to pass the time while in Sorrento.

I rubbed the aching spot on my chest and again felt the locket beneath my fingers. Several times I was tempted to throw it away—but didn't. Some perverse part of me still believed he'd never intended to leave me like that. Was I a romantic idiot?

Since then the pain has lessened, though I vowed never to fall for a guy that easily again. Lesson learned.

I shook off the memory and glanced around, trying to see past the hordes of students. Many of them bumped into me in their eagerness to reach friends or the crowded stalls. Then I saw it—a red and white striped marquee with the sign: Historical Society. Pictures of old houses, archaeological sites, even weapons—replicas, I assumed—adorned the poles and display tables. The two guys and one girl behind the counter wore period costume.

Seeing an opening, I pressed through the crowd and tripped over the rope that secured the marquee to the ground peg. A pair of strong arms reached down and caught me.

'Hey, you okay?' A deep, male voice asked. A tall, brown haired guy dressed as a Viking looked down at me, smiling. His grey eyes were ringed with blue.

'Yeah, fine, thanks.' I tried to keep my voice level to hide my embarrassment.

'I kinda like the idea of a girl falling for me!' He grinned and the pupils in his eyes expanded almost obscuring the grey.

'That the best line you got?' I tried not to laugh as I brushed down my shorts.

'Nah, heaps more, even worse than that one.' His face lit up as he laughed—so infectious I couldn't help but join in. 'My name's Tim.'

'I'm Laura.'

'This yours?' He bent and picked up my locket from the grass.

'Um, thanks.' The clasp was broken, and for a fleeting moment, as I peered at it, Philippe's face appeared in my mind. I pushed the image aside, and slipped the locket into my short's pocket.

'Would've been a pity to have lost it. It's beautiful,' Tim said, 'like you.'

His compliment caught me off guard. Philippe had called me beautiful. *That ache in my chest again.* I looked away and mumbled a quick thanks.

'Look, I'm just about to break for lunch? Join me?'

I leafed through the information leaflets scattered on the table. 'I'm, uh… not sure. I'm supposed to meet a friend here.'

'Okay, I should've known.' I heard the disappointment in his voice.

I smiled as I guessed what he must be thinking and glanced up at him. 'Girlfriend. My bestie.'

His face brightened. 'Crazy-orange-skirt, girl?'

I'm sure my eyes widened. 'How did—'

'Couldn't miss that! Saw you next to her, and I hoped you'd head this way.' He grinned again. 'Didn't think you'd literally fall into my arms though.'

I rolled my eyes then scanned the table again, this time for the registration sheet. 'Where do I sign up?'

'Uh, here.' He handed me a form.

As I filled it out and checked the activities schedule, Tim moved away. I glanced up as he removed his cloak and brown tunic, and slipped on a T-shirt. His back faced me and I got a good view of his wide shoulders. He had mentioned a lunch break, and I wondered whether walking around campus dressed as a Viking could get you beaten up.

He was an attractive guy, but in a different way from Philippe. But then, few men could compare physically to him.

Argh! I shook my head to dislodge his image from my mind. I had an hour before I was to meet Angie, so it couldn't do any harm to accept Tim's lunch invitation. Besides, it was time to put Philippe behind me.

Tim said something to another attendant, a girl dressed in a Jane Austin-style dress, who handed out information leaflets. She nodded and alerted the other attendant, a guy dressed as a Roman soldier.

'Yeah, mate—go,' the guy said to Tim before going back to demonstrating the use of a sword to several admiring male students.

'Tim,' I said. 'That lunch offer still on?'

His beaming smile gave me the answer. 'So, what are you majoring in?' he asked as we walked off the green to the Student Union Building.

'Dip Ed,' I said. 'I think I'll enjoy teaching little kids.'

He nodded. 'Nice. I'm doing honours in Archaeology.'

There was a vacant table at one of the cafes on the ground floor. 'Are there any jobs in that?' I asked.

'Soon find out.'

We ordered Thai, sat down and talked. His grey eyes sparkled when he spoke of going on digs, here and overseas. 'I need several seasons of fieldwork to qualify. Then maybe go for an academic position.'

'Don't you need a PhD for that?'

'Yup. It's gonna be a long haul.' He lifted his polystyrene coffee cup in mock salute.

I smiled, wished him the best, and it occurred to me, that I really hoped he'd achieve it. That surprised me. I was beginning to like this guy, but I had no intention of developing any deeper feelings. I would concentrate on my studies, enjoy new friendships and immerse myself in university life.

Yet there was something appealing about Tim, the animated way he spoke about life, his funny anecdotes and the silly pick-up lines he told me he'd used. As he talked, I laughed till my sides ached.

I glanced at my watch. Where had that hour gone? 'Oops, gotta go.'

'Can I see you again? Here's my number.' He extracted a pocket notebook, scribbled something down, ripped a sheet out and handed it to me. 'Call me. Please.'

I scribbled mine on a paper napkin and passed it to him. 'Likewise.'

Back at the marquee, we said goodbye—for now—and I met up with Angie.

'Ex-cell-ent!' she said after I told her about Tim. 'Go for it, Laura. I've been so worried about you, mooning over that other guy. Forget him and move on.'

'I have.' *I really have.*

At home that afternoon, I pulled out Philippe's locket and gazed at it. That familiar ache I'd lived with for the last four weeks surfaced for a moment, but with far less intensity.

Since the clasp was broken, I tied a knot in the chain and hung it on my dresser mirror, to dangle there with my other accessories. It would be a constant reminder not to give my heart away so easily—the pain was too great. It would take a special man for me to ever fall in love again.

I heard the hallway phone ring. A few seconds later Mum called up to me. 'Laura? Do you know someone called Tim?'

'Goodbye Philippe,' I whispered as I closed my bedroom door and dashed down the stairs.

***

Four weeks earlier....

PHILIPPE

Philippe paced in front of his master's desk and checked his watch for the umpteenth time. He shouldn't be here. Laura would be waiting for him in the hotel foyer wondering where he was.

He hadn't fed either, and that exacerbated his edginess. The sweet tang of blood from the humans strolling in the courtyard below drifted in from the open window, torturing his senses. He ran his tongue over his extended incisors.

The door opened, and his master, Lord Lucien, strode in. The grim set to his jaw would've had any other of his kind sweating with fear. The nearly two-thousand-year-old leader of his clan never hesitated to kill any who interfered with his plans.

But Philippe wasn't interfering. On the contrary, he was hastening them. A shadow of a smile curved the edges of his mouth. Perhaps his master might even thank him for this.

Still, Lord Lucien was unpredictable.

Philippe bowed, as Lucien seated himself in the red leather chair behind his desk, his sharp, narrow-eyed gaze like an x-ray penetrating into the darkest corners of Philippe's mind.

'I don't recall giving you permission to approach Laura.' The deadly edge to his voice had Philippe clenching his fists.

'She was being harassed by a bunch of human boys. I … simply stepped in.'

Lucien interlaced his fingers on the top of the desk, twirling his thumbs as he stared at Philippe. 'Jake or Cal could've done that.'

Her unseen bodyguards. Laura was unaware of the protective ring around her, nor why they were there. 'They were too slow.'

Lucien raised an eyebrow. 'Or perhaps you were too quick to interfere. Now why would you do that?'

Because I have every right to see her, he felt like saying, but the dangerous tone in Lucien's voice warned him to be cautious. 'I … couldn't help myself.' Which was the truth.

Lucien sighed loudly. 'How old are you, Jean?'

His mother had christened him Jean-Philippe Louis Auguste Reynard. Everyone just called him Jean. He preferred Philippe. And Lucien knew exactly how old he was.

'Over one-hundred-and-eighty, my lord.'

'Mmmm. Old enough for self-control, don't you think?'

Philippe wanted to roll his eyes. 'Yes, my lord.'

'Then why didn't you leave it there, instead of enticing her to meet you night after night and inflaming her feelings for you? I welcomed you into my household, and this is how you repay me?'

Philippe's blood chilled. He swallowed.

Lucien stood. 'You know what she is and why she's out of bounds to all our kind until her coming of age. Both Jake and Cal warned you, yet you ignored them and continued seeing her.'

'My lord, I meant no disrespect.'

Philippe thought back to the other night, meeting Laura in the foyer. It was his damn curiosity, and an invitation from Jake, that had tempted him to journey to Sorrento and see the girl he'd known as a child during a four-year stay in Sydney. But that girl was no longer a child. At eighteen, her beauty surpassed any other woman he'd ever known, and coupled with her refreshing innocence, he had to have her.

He'd wanted her to himself all night, but Jake had threatened to drag him out unless he took her back to her room. It'd rankled him they'd been under observation the entire time. Even hiding out in the lonely fisherman's hut had only been a temporary escape. They had been followed. So Philippe had to make sure he had Laura's heart, knowing his behaviour would be reported, and thus a matter of time before Lucien himself intervened.

And here he was.

'Give me a good reason not to punish you.'

'Because of my bloodline.'

Lucien's eyes narrowed into slits, and he leaned forward on the desk. 'Go on.'

Philippe wanted to savour this moment, to remember it always as the night his master would thank him. 'You know that my mother was Adelaide, daughter of the Duke D'Orleans.'

Lucien nodded.

'My father was the Duke of Atholl. His blood is Pict.' Philippe allowed himself a tiny smile.

Lucien's expression didn't change. 'Your mother told you this?'

'On her deathbed.'

Lucien spun around to face the window behind his desk, arms clasped behind his back. Reflected in the dark glass, his face remained inscrutable. Another reason most of their kind treaded warily around him — nothing about his master betrayed his thoughts. One never really knew where they stood with him. Only those closest to him knew the true Lucien Lebrettan, or 'Luc' to those in his immediate circle. And although Philippe was regarded as one of the clan — by proxy — he felt he never truly *belonged*.

Perhaps now, that could change.

'She returns your affection?'

'Yes, I'm sure of it.'

Lucien's shoulders lifted in a huffed laugh. 'Laura's only eighteen. Still a child in many ways. Inexperienced, innocent, naive … no idea what being in love is. You will not be the first she'll believe herself in love with.' He laughed again.

Philippe's fingers curled into a tight fist. As far as he was concerned, there would be no other men in her life. She was meant for him. 'My lord, by right of my blood, I wish to lay claim to Laura when she comes of age.'

'She's not meant for you.'

'How can you say that?'

'There's another, with a truer claim.'

Philippe's stomach clenched. 'Who?'

Lucien angled his head to the side, a snarl curling the edges of his mouth. 'Are you questioning me?'

Philippe knew better than to press the point. 'No … my lord.'

Lucien sighed and turned to face him fully. 'It's enough for you to know that I don't believe you have a legitimate claim. Besides,' he continued, 'according to our laws, Laura must decide for herself at her coming-of-age. If she still loves you then, as you say she does now, you may assert your claim before the assembly.' He slammed one hand on the table, and with the other stabbed a pointed finger in his direction. 'But, until that time, I forbid you to see her or be in contact with her. You're to return to Paris immediately.'

Philippe's mouth dried. He'd been sure his claim would be acknowledged, and even … welcomed. How had this happened? Now to be told he must not see her for years? Every part of his being revolted against it. She was waiting for him even now, in this same building, five floors down. He could hear her voice, her concern that he wasn't there.

Every fibre of his being longed to go to her, and the struggle to remain silent, to obey his master even as his will rebelled at the unfair command imposed on him, was excruciating. Every muscle in his body tensed, his fists clenched so tightly, his nails would leave permanent marks in his skin.

Yet, it was unthinkable to disobey his master.

It meant death.

Philippe shook his head, barely able to utter the words. 'She'll think I've stood her up. That I don't care for her.'

Lucien moved around the desk, strode to the door and opened it. 'She's young and will recover soon enough. Cal will escort you to my jet.'

Philippe's gut churned even as anger surged through his veins heating his cheeks and forcing his blood to whoosh loudly in his ears, drowning out all other sounds. 'At least let me leave her a note … a message. Please, my lord!'

'Don't keep my pilot waiting.' Lucien waved toward the outer door.

Just disappear, without leaving a word? Bile rose in his throat and, for a split second, he considered pushing past Cal and running down to the foyer, to let Laura know he wasn't abandoning her.

The punishment he'd receive would be worth it.

As if reading his thoughts, Lucien gripped his arm, and together with Cal, marched him to the service elevator. His unnatural strength was no match against the combined power of two of his kind.

Defeated, a shroud of humiliation smothering him and chafing on his every nerve, Philippe hung his head as they led him out, the pressure of their grip on his arms biting deep.

In the basement car park, a black limousine waited. Its green-uniformed driver held the door open as Cal bundled him into the back seat. Seated next to him — in case he'd try and do a runner, Philippe thought — Cal signalled the driver.

The car surged forward and they sped out to Sorrento's dark and deserted streets.

As they passed the train station, the loud guffaws of several youths caught Philippe's attention. One voice, in particular, he recognised. A snarl escaped his lips. There he was, the youth who'd harassed Laura and whose fault it was that Philippe was in this humiliating position. If not for him….

'I haven't fed.'

'There are blood bags on the plane.'

'I need to hunt.' *To teach that peasant boy a lesson.*

He knew Cal would understand. Their kind lived for the hunt, the thrill of the chase and then … the kill. Although the latter was forbidden. Humans were a protected species. Pity on this one occasion he wasn't allowed to make an exception.

Cal signalled the driver to stop. 'Twenty minutes max, Jean.'

With the collar of his black leather jacket pulled high against the back of his neck, Philippe stepped out of the car, a grim smile plastered on his face. Blending in with the dark, he approached the lads. Only his eyes would betray his presence, the pale lavender orbs all but glowing with the rush that came with stalking prey.

Their raucous laughter stopped when he neared. Two of the lads crossed themselves, cried out "vampiro" and ran off into the dark. Only his prey, whose gaze he had captured, remained still, eyes wide in his ashen face.

Philippe grabbed the back of the lad's neck and angled his head to expose the soft skin of his throat. A golden crucifix glinted up at him. Swiping it to the side, Philippe allowed himself a savoury sniff before biting down hard. No numbing vampire saliva this time. He wanted this one to feel the pain, satisfaction humming through him when the lad screamed and struggled to free himself.

He would've kept feeding, taking larger and larger gulps until the lad's heart slowed and eventually stuttered to a halt, if not for Cal's grip on his shoulder.

'Enough. Let him go.'

Philippe loosened his hold. The lad slid to the ground, droplets of blood smearing his padded coat. Philippe wiped his mouth with the back of his hand, spun on his heel and returned to the car while Cal mesmerized the lad into forgetfulness. Apart from two strange marks on his neck, the lad would have no memory of the encounter.

In some ways, he was lucky. If Philippe could erase the memory of Laura from his mind, it would be a mercy. But such a thought was akin to blasphemy. A fierce resolve possessed him, such that nothing would keep him from Laura's side, even if it meant leaving his beloved Paris and moving to Sydney to be near her, as close and yet as unseen as her preternatural bodyguards.

And when the time came, he would remind Lucien of their bargain.

Laura would be his.

THE END ... for now

www.ingramcontent.com/pod-product-compliance
Lightning Source LLC
Chambersburg PA
CBHW030439120726
47903CB00003B/1036